This book belongs to:

_____

_____

For Peyton and Weston —

May you enjoy the miracle of Christmas each year,

as I enjoy the miracle of you.

www.reindeerinhere.com
www.adamreed.com

REINDEER IN HERE®

A Christmas Friend

Written By
Adam Reed

Illustrated By
Izzy Bean

Dear friendly grown-up,
In early December please give me
to a special child and then
read them this Christmas tale.
Sincerely,
Reindeer In Here

Once a year, in the month of December,
a special time comes that we all must remember.

It's not Christmas day,
although that's great, too.

Today is a day
meant just for you.

There're still a few weeks until Christmas is here
but Santa's sent your first gift—it's ME, your reindeer.

Since I'm from the North Pole, I'm used to the cold,

but I love hugs and warm cuddles; they're better than gold.

I also like cocoa and candy canes galore.

Oh, and socks on my hooves!

Do you want to hear more?

I am a bit different and my friends are, too.

We're quirky and special, just like you.

My best friend is a snowman with a candy-cane nose.

He's quite a sight.

Have you seen one of those?

There's also Peeky, who's not like most polar bears.
Unlike his brothers, he only has three little hairs.

And finally, Cecilia the seal with a permanent smile

and two cross-eyed penguins
who haven't walked straight in a while.

Friends are special. Friends are fun.
You get a Christmas friend today,
and I'm the one!

I'm your Christmas pal
and I've come a long way,

with a story from Santa,
I have something to say.

A long time ago when Santa first delivered toys,
he didn't know the true wishes of all the girls and boys.

A world filled with children, yet only some wrote him a letter.
He wanted a way to know each child even better.

So Santa looked to his reindeer and proudly they stood.
He knew they would help him any way that they could.

In a sea of antlers, Santa asked one and all,
"How do we learn their Christmas wish—
why that's an order quite tall!"

The reindeer started to whisper, but not one spoke aloud . . .
until a head quite unusual popped up in the crowd.

You see, two equal antlers are normal.
One smaller is not.
This little reindeer was different,
and came forth with a thought.

"Although we're all reindeer,
and look somewhat the same,
like children we're different,
beyond just our name."

"To be different is normal. I've got one antler small.
Thinking different will fix this problem
once and for all!"

The reindeer looked at each other,
and saw it was true,
the smallest of them all
knew what to do.

"Santa, you have reindeer that travel and roam.
We can help guide you to each child's home,
not only by lifting and pulling your sleigh,
we'll go a little early and with the children we'll stay."

This little reindeer's idea was something quite new.
Santa listened closely. What would he do?

Then Santa smiled big,
all dressed in red
while a new way
to know children
danced in his head.

"Why didn't I think of that?" cried jolly Kris Kringle.
Then the reindeer jumped around with bells all a-jingle.

"Each child will get a reindeer to name.
The month of December will never be the same!"

"From here on out, this is how it will be.
You will become my ears and eyes to see."

He bent toward his reindeer, "This is what I need you to do:
Go find a child and stay all the month through."

"When you get to their house let them show you around—
a new place each morning. How does that sound?"

"You should discover where they eat, sleep, and play,
and what their true wishes are for Christmas Day."

And so it began
and now continues for you.
That's why I'm here.
We've got so much to do.

I'm little for a reason,
so take me everywhere—
each day a new place
and adventures to share.

I don't talk a lot but that's all right.
With some holiday magic,
I'll report back to Santa each night.

Then, when Santa finally
arrives to deliver the toys,
we reindeer will tell him about
our good girls and good boys!

On Christmas Eve, put me next to the tree
and I will show Santa all he should see.

As Santa delivers each gift from his sleigh,
the other reindeer will join him
and we'll be off on our way.

So please be a good friend and always kiss me goodnight . . .

and on Christmas morning,
you'll see a great sight.

Wishes fulfilled and lots to unwrap.
Your reindeer won't be here, but in a year I'll be back.

Why do I leave you on Christmas Day?
To get Santa back to the North Pole by guiding his sleigh.

Each reindeer is different, and each child is too.
The Christmas magic begins now! Let's get to know you.

Be good boys and good girls all through the year,
and enjoy this time with your magical reindeer.

West on
Jennifer
Jonathan
Peyton
Lincoln
Naomi
Laura
Jaxson
Damian

A new family tradition meant just for you.
It's time to have fun—what should we do?

I'm your reindeer, please give me a name.
I promise your December will never be the same!

This reindeer's name is:

_____